Elisha:
A Man of Gentleness
& Self-Control

Written By: Rediesha C. Allen

Illustrated By: Hatice Bayramoglu

Series Editors: Reginald Robinson; Lenny Williams, & Shiree Fowler

Library of Congress Control Number: 2021942383

ISBN: 978-1-62676-495-8 hardback

ISBN: 978-1-62676-496-5 paperback

ISBN: 978-1-62676-497-2 ebook

This book is dedicated to my Lord and Savior, Jesus Christ. Thank you for guiding me since I was born into this world.

To my husband, Akil. Thank you for following Jesus with your whole heart. I love you forevermore. Forever I Do!!

To my amazingly courageous daughters, Marlee Elise and Crystal Chinel. I live to make you proud. I love you to the moon and back!

To every little girl and boy who will read this book. Dream big and pray. The Lord will guide you!

Rediesha C. Allen

Meet Elisha! A gentle and wise man who always showed self-control.

1

Elisha became known and respected as a mighty prophet of God by many people, but his story did not begin here at the Jordan River.

Long ago, as Elisha was tending to the needs of his oxen, he noticed a man approaching from a distance.

3

He did not know the man, but Elisha was about to discover that God had a very special assignment for him. Elisha had been chosen by God!

The man who visited Elisha was the Prophet Elijah. The Lord chose Elijah to teach Elisha to be the best leader he could be, so he gave Elisha a special mantle to wear as a symbol of God's calling.

One day, a very poor woman came to him. She was sad and needed money for her family.

Elisha responded with gentleness and self-control by telling her to get as many jars as she could find to fill with oil.

11

The woman knew she did not have much oil, but she did as Elisha told her and God blessed her obedience! As she poured, all the jars were filled with oil so that she could sell them for money she desperately needed!

Through God's power, Elisha performed many miracles. At one time, he prayed for a husband and wife to have a son.

The son became sick a few years later, but Elisha returned to pray for him and he was healed.

14

After Elisha paused and prayed, he told the soldier to wash seven times in the Jordan river. The soldier listened and was healed! What a miracle!

16

With God's power, Elisha traveled
many places and helped many people.

17

As God's prophet, Elisha earned the respect of many, but the only thing that mattered to him was his obedience to God's will. The same obedience he had in the fields with his oxen.

Remember that you, also, have the ability to pause and pray just like Elisha. Ask the Lord to fill all of your thoughts with gentleness and self-control.

19

When you do, you show the power of God through your actions!

Dear God,

Thank you for this day. Please help me to make good choices. When I am angry, help me to be gentle and to have self-control. I want people to see You through my actions. Amen

Order Melanin Origins
ALL In All Series!

www.MelaninOrigins.com

CPSIA information can be obtained
at www.ICGtesting.com
Printed in the USA
BVHW092043121021
618772BV00002B/70